RAIN FORESTS

by
Joanna Brundle

Photo Credits

Images are courtesy of Shutterstock.com. With thanks to Getty Images, Thinkstock Photo and iStockphoto.

Cover – Chansom Pantip, 4&5 – Sorn340 Images, eAlisa, bogadeva1983, reisegraf.ch, Banach Ewelina, 6&7 – Kirasolly, Nowaczyk, Ondrej Prosicky, feathercollector, 8&9 – KayaMe, Ondrej Prosicky, Alessandro Pierpaoli, pisces2386, Tonio_75, 10&11 – Dr Morley Read, Shulevskyy Volodymyr, Ondrej Prosicky, Pedro Helder Pinheiro, 12&13 – SL-Photography, Ryan M. Bolton, Paman Aheri, Juhku, 14&15 – Kagai19927, Usanee, Jeff Holcombe, Josanel Sugasti, Ryan M. Bolton, 16&17 – Anna Veselova, dvigalet, Cristian Gusa, Dennis van de Water, Kevin Wells Photography, 18&19 – Ghing, Warawich Suyasa, Babu Paul, Erik Zandboer, 20&21 –Yatra, BestForBest, Heike Rau, 22&23 – Gustavo Frazao, fivespots, Hand Denis Schneider, Toniflap, buteo, 24&25 – Thammanoon Khamchalee, Rich Carey, Alex East, Roman Rybaleov, 26&27 – FloridaStock, Alexandros Michailidis, Jeroen Mikkers, 28&29 – K I Photography, dolphfyn, Dennis Wegewijs, Rob Crandall, 30&31 – gary yim, massdon, sma1050.

Published in 2022 by The Rosen Publishing Group, Inc.
29 East 21st Street, New York, NY 10010

©2020 BookLife Publishing Ltd.

Edited by:
William Anthony

Designed by:
Gareth Liddington

Cataloging-in-Publication Data

Names: Brundle, Joanna.
Title: Rain forests / Joanna Brundle.
Description: New York : PowerKids Press, 2022. | Series: Discover and learn | Includes glossary and index.
Identifiers: ISBN 9781502661999 (pbk.) | ISBN 9781502662019 (library bound) | ISBN 9781502662002 (6 pack) | ISBN 9781502662026 (ebook)
Subjects: LCSH: Rain forests--Juvenile literature. | Rain forest ecology--Juvenile literature.
Classification: LCC QH541.5.R27 B78 2022 | DDC 577.34--dc23

All rights reserved. No part of this book may be reproduced in any form without permission in writing from the publisher, except by a reviewer.

Manufactured in the United States of America

CPSIA Compliance Information: Batch #CSPK22. For Further Information contact Rosen Publishing, New York, New York at 1-800-237-9932.

Find us on

CONTENTS

*Words that look like **this** are explained in the glossary on page 31.*

Page 4	What Are Rain Forests?
Page 6	Let's Take a Closer Look
Page 7	Emergent Layer
Page 8	The Canopy
Page 10	The Understory
Page 12	The Forest Floor
Page 14	Adapting to Rain Forest Life
Page 18	After Dark
Page 20	Rain Forest Resources
Page 22	The Amazon Rain Forest
Page 24	Threats to Rain Forests
Page 26	Rain Forests and Global Warming
Page 28	Rain Forest Recovery
Page 30	Fascinating Facts
Page 31	Glossary
Page 32	Index

WHAT ARE RAIN FORESTS?

Tropical rain forests are hot, **humid** forests that grow near the equator, in an area known as the tropics. They cover only a tiny amount of Earth, but they are home to over half of Earth's animal and plant **species**.

Mammals such as sloths and monkeys, **reptiles** such as snakes and chameleons, birds such as eagles and parrots, and insects such as ants and butterflies all live in rain forests. Thousands of species of trees, flowering plants, shrubs, and ferns provide food for plant eaters that, in turn, provide food for meat eaters.

COLORFUL RAIN FOREST ORCHIDS

HOWLER MONKEY

Rain forests have been around for millions of years, since the time of the dinosaurs. Tropical rain forests receive strong sunlight and very heavy rainfall of over 70 inches (1,800 mm) a year. Temperatures are very warm throughout the year, rarely falling below 68 degrees Fahrenheit (20 degrees Celsius), even at night.

The world's largest tropical rain forests are the Amazon rain forest in South America and the Congolese rain forest in Africa. Australia has a small rain forest in Queensland, and in Asia the largest rain forest stretches across Indonesia.

RAIN FORESTS PROVIDE A RANGE OF HABITATS FROM THE FOREST FLOOR UP TO THE HIGHEST BRANCHES.

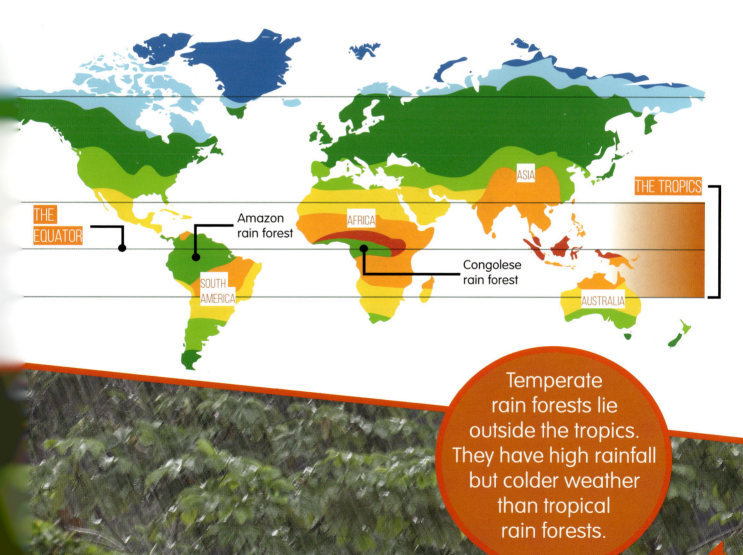

Temperate rain forests lie outside the tropics. They have high rainfall but colder weather than tropical rain forests.

LET'S TAKE A CLOSER LOOK

Rain forests are made up of different layers. Each has its own plant and animal species that are **adapted** to the different amounts of sunlight and rainfall reaching each layer.

EMERGENT LAYER
CANOPY LAYER
UNDERSTORY LAYER
FOREST FLOOR

KAPOK TREES ARE FOUND IN THE EMERGENT LAYER.

Unlike animals, plants are able to make their own food, which they need in order to live and grow. They make food using water, **carbon dioxide** from the air, and sunlight. In the rain forest, plants compete for sunlight. Only the strongest trees reach the highest level, known as the emergent layer. This layer receives bright sunshine all year round and is also very hot and windy.

EMERGENT LAYER

The tallest trees in the emergent layer can grow over 230 feet (70 m) tall. They have wide, spreading tops and tough, waxy leaves that give protection from the sunlight. The strong winds and height from the forest floor help scatter the seeds of these trees. They also make the emergent layer a dangerous place to live.

SCARLET MACAWS NEST IN HOLES IN TREES IN THE EMERGENT LAYER. THEY EAT INSECTS, FRUITS, SEEDS, AND NUTS.

The emergent layer is home to all sorts of animals, such as monkeys, bats, butterflies, and the smallest bird on Earth, the hummingbird.

Harpy eagles build their nests in the tops of emergent layer trees, giving them a good view of their **prey** below.

7

THE CANOPY

THE THICK CANOPY LAYER STOPS MOST OF THE SUNLIGHT FROM REACHING THE UNDERSTORY LAYER.

The canopy is made up of trees that reach a height of about 130 feet (40 m). Their leaves and branches spread out to form a thick canopy, like a giant umbrella, that shades the layers underneath.

Many animals, such as this squirrel monkey, take shelter in the canopy from forest floor **predators**. Some never come down to the forest floor.

Thanks to the plentiful rain and sunlight reaching the canopy, there is lots of food for the many species that live here, including squirrel monkeys, tree frogs, bats, and snakes. From the air, the canopy looks like a continuous layer. However, most trees do not touch one another and animals have to fly, glide, or leap between them.

SQUIRREL MONKEY

8

Thick, climbing vines called lianas are common in the canopy. They begin life on the ground, but then attach themselves to trees and climb upward in search of sunlight. Lianas often become tangled together, forming networks and pathways that animals use to help them move around.

LIANAS LOOK LIKE ROPES HANGING IN THE RAIN FOREST. THEY CAN GROW TO HUNDREDS OF FEET IN LENGTH.

Some beautiful flowering plants, such as orchids and bromeliads, are not attached to the ground. They grow on other plants instead. They are common in the canopy. Some plants, such as the strangler fig, eventually smother and kill the tree that supports them.

The thick, waxy leaves of a bromeliad form a bowl shape that catches water and gives a home to frogs, snails, and beetles.

STRANGLER FIG

THE UNDERSTORY

The hot, humid understory is quite dark because it only gets a small amount of sunlight. The plants that grow here often have large, dark-green leaves to catch as much sunlight as possible. They include small trees, low-lying shrubs, ferns, climbing plants, and bananas.

Mosses, **fungi**, and **algae** grow on tree trunks and branches. If a canopy tree dies and falls over, understory trees can grow very quickly to fill in the gap. The few flowering plants are often brightly colored or strong smelling to attract bees and butterflies.

BRIGHTLY COLORED HELICONIA

The understory has perfect conditions for the insects that live there, including bees, stick insects, moths, and butterflies. These insects are food for birds, bats, monkeys, frogs, and lizards.

THERE IS VERY LITTLE WIND IN THE UNDERSTORY TO SCATTER THE SEEDS OF PLANTS. SEEDS ARE SPREAD ON THE BODIES AND IN THE DUNG (POOP) OF ANIMALS.

GLASSWING BUTTERFLY

The pattern of a jaguar's coat helps it blend into its surroundings until it is ready to pounce.

The understory's humidity also makes it an ideal habitat for creatures such as tree frogs and salamanders that need to stop their moist skin from drying out. Understory trees are home to large predators such as jaguars. They wait on the lookout in the branches and hunt at night.

THE FOREST FLOOR

FUNGI

The forest floor is very shady as little sunlight reaches this layer. It is, however, a very important part of the rain forest because this is where decomposition (rotting) takes place. The dark, moist floor means dead plants and animals that have fallen down will rot quickly. Fungi and **microorganisms** recycle and feed on **nutrients** from the rotting material, beginning the **food chain**. Termites, spiders, cockroaches, and centipedes also live on the forest floor.

Scorpions feed on insects and spiders.

The forest floor is where some of the rain forest's largest animals are found. Depending on where the rain forest is, these animals might include tigers, pumas, ocelots, tapirs, armadillos, and warthogs.

Tigers live in the tropical rain forests of South Asia.

BUTTRESS TREE ROOTS

Rain forest soil is poor with nutrients only found near the surface. Tree roots are usually shallow. This can make trees unstable, so some produce buttress roots. These roots grow out from the trunk, as much as 15 feet (4.5 m) above the ground, and support the tree. They also spread out around the bottom of the tree, helping it reach soil nutrients farther away.

ADAPTING TO RAIN FOREST LIFE

All living things have to adapt to their environment in order to survive. Every habitat is home to plants and animals that are specially adapted to live there. The leaves of canopy plants have pointed ends, called drip tips, that help rainwater to run off them easily. Without this adaptation, the leaves would quickly rot.

DRIP TIP

PITCHER PLANTS

The smell of the pitcher plants' nectar attracts insects. The insects fall into the nectar and become the pitcher plants' food. Inside each pitcher are small hairs that point downward to stop the insects from escaping.

Sloths are very well **camouflaged** and move extremely slowly, making them very difficult for predators to spot. They spend so much of their time asleep or perfectly still that algae can grow on their fur. The green color of the algae provides extra camouflage. Sloths can turn their heads almost all the way round, helping them spot predators.

Sloths use their strong claws to cling to tree branches.

The flying frog is adapted to move easily around the canopy. It has webbed hands and feet and a flap of loose skin that stretches between its limbs when it jumps, so it can glide between branches.

The toucan is a colorful canopy bird. Its long bill helps it reach fruit on branches that would be too weak for it to stand on and that other birds cannot reach. The bill also has a sawlike edge that helps the toucan grasp its food and peel fruit. It can also use its bill to control its body temperature, so it does not overheat.

THE TOUCAN'S COLORS PROVIDE CAMOUFLAGE IN THE LIGHT OF THE CANOPY.

Aye-ayes tap on trees using their long middle fingers. They then listen for bugs moving under the bark and use their long middle fingers to scoop them out.

AYE-AYES ALSO USE THEIR LONG FINGERS TO EAT COCONUTS AND FRUITS.

16

The blue morpho butterfly has many adaptations that help it survive. A flash of its bright blue wings startles predators. The large eyespots on the underside of its wings may trick predators into thinking it is a much larger animal.

EYESPOTS

Leafcutter ants are adapted to carry things many times heavier than themselves. They bite leaves into pieces that they carry back to their nests underground. They then feed on fungus that grows on the leaves.

AFTER DARK

Nocturnal animals are those that are mainly active during the night. They sleep during the day and hunt or feed after dark. At night, rain forests are teeming with nocturnal creatures, including moths, owls, armadillos, and some types of snakes and beetles.

THE ATLAS MOTH IS ONE OF THE BIGGEST INSECTS, WITH A WINGSPAN OF UP TO 12 INCHES (30 CM).

Some nocturnal creatures, such as tarsiers, have huge eyes that help them see in dim light. Each of the tarsier's eyes can weigh as much as its brain. Tarsiers also have excellent hearing. They move their large ears constantly to help them find their prey in the dark.

The emerald tree boa is a nocturnal predator that lives in the canopy. By day, it loops itself around tree branches, but at night, it creeps up on its prey, pounces, and then squeezes its victim to death.

Emerald tree boas are carnivores (meat eaters) that eat lizards, frogs, squirrels, and small monkeys.

THE EMERALD TREE BOA CAN LAST WEEKS WITHOUT A MEAL.

Flying foxes are found in rain forests in Madagascar, Australia, and Asia.

Flying foxes, also known as fox bats, have wide leathery wings and fox-like faces. They live in huge groups called colonies, hanging upside down in trees by day. At night, they use their excellent sight and sense of smell to find the fruits, nectar, and flowers that they like to eat.

19

RAIN FOREST RESOURCES

Resources are valuable or useful items. Many natural resources, such as rubber, are found in rain forests.

Rubber is made from a milky, white liquid called latex, taken from rubber trees.

COCOA PODS CONTAIN SEEDS THAT ARE USED TO MAKE COCOA BUTTER, WHICH IS FOUND IN cosmetics, CANDLES, AND CHOCOLATE.

FOODS

Foods found in rain forests include fruits such as bananas, acai berries, and pineapples. There are also spices such as vanilla, black pepper, and cinnamon, and nuts including cashews and Brazil nuts. Coffee plants also grow in rain forests, along with cocoa trees.

WOOD

Rain forests contain many valuable hardwood trees, such as teak and mahogany. Wood from these trees is used to make furniture and flooring.

MEDICINE

Rain forest plants are used as ingredients in some of the most important medicines. This includes medicines for heart disease, malaria, fever, and pain. Rain forest plants are also used to make antiseptics, which are used to clean wounds.

Quinine, a medicine used to treat malaria, is found in cinchona tree bark, which grows in Africa and South America.

Many antibiotics, used to treat infection, are made using rain forest plants. Some antibiotics are becoming less effective because they have been used too much. Fortunately, scientists think that, thanks to the huge range of plants in the rain forests, more antibiotics will be discovered.

THE AMAZON RAIN FOREST

A SQUARE MILE IS AN AREA THAT MEASURES ONE MILE IN WIDTH AND LENGTH.

The Amazon rain forest in South America is the world's largest tropical rain forest. It covers an area of 2.3 million square miles (6 million sq km). The rain forest takes its name from the Amazon River, a network of waterways that stretch 4,000 miles (6,400 km).

Different peoples living in the Amazon rain forest each have their own language and culture. Some have never had contact with the outside world.

FOREST PEOPLES

Groups of indigenous people have lived in the Amazon rain forest for thousands of years. There are some groups that rely on the rain forest for all their needs, including food, medicine, and clothes.

The Amazon rain forest is home to thousands of animal species, including one of the world's largest spiders – the Goliath birdeater. It feeds on mice, earthworms, frogs, and birds. This spider injects poison into its victim using its long fangs.

GOLIATH BIRDEATER

Capybaras live in groups along riverbanks. Capybara young are sometimes eaten by caimans that hide in the river. Other animals that live in the river include manatees, red-bellied piranha fish, which have razor-sharp teeth, and dolphins.

CAPYBARAS

The black caiman can reach up to 16 feet (5 m) in length, more than two times an average human's height.

BLACK CAIMAN

23

THREATS TO RAIN FORESTS

Rain forests are under threat due to deforestation – the cutting down and removal of trees from a forested area. More than half the world's rain forests have already been destroyed to provide timber and space for farming, mining, and building.

EVERY HOUR, AN AREA OF RAIN FOREST THE SIZE OF 1,800 FOOTBALL FIELDS IS CUT DOWN.

CAN YOU SEE WHERE THE RAIN FOREST HAS BEEN CUT DOWN?

FARMING

Farming is one of the biggest reasons for deforestation. As worldwide demand for food grows, rain forests are being cut down and burned to make way for cattle ranches and crops, such as corn and soybeans. Huge palm plantations have also replaced rain forests. Palm oil is used in many products including shampoo, pizzas, and peanut butter.

MINING

Large areas of rain forest have been removed, especially in the Amazon basin, to allow mining of metals, such as copper, iron, gold, and tin. Miners and loggers clear even more land to build roads to move their materials around. Mining also causes pollution and soil damage that makes it hard for trees to regrow.

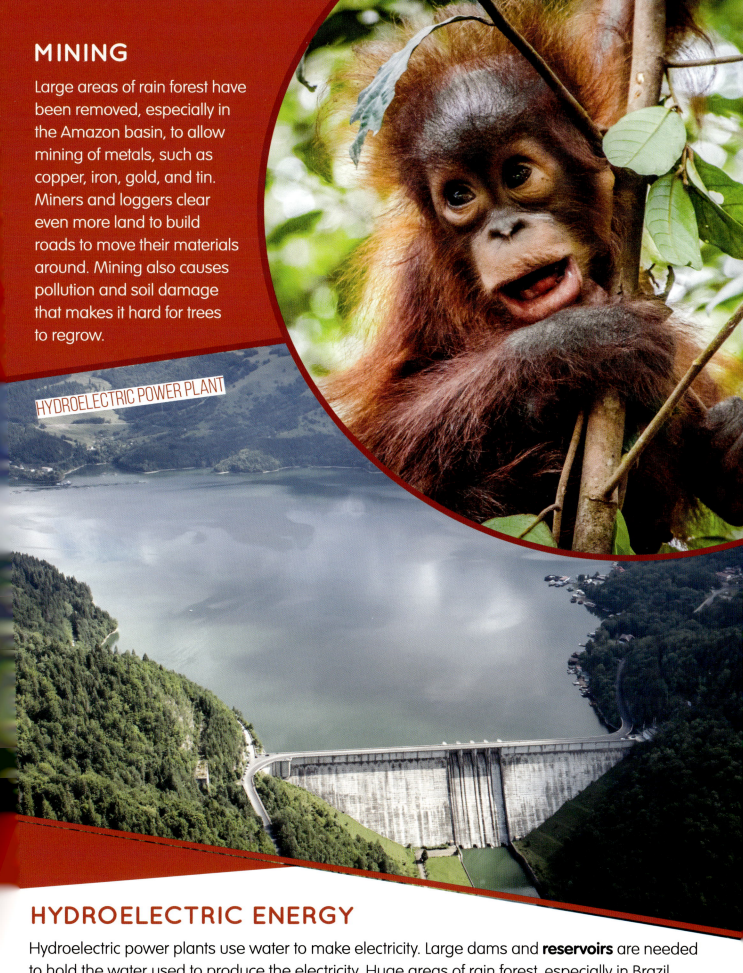

HYDROELECTRIC POWER PLANT

HYDROELECTRIC ENERGY

Hydroelectric power plants use water to make electricity. Large dams and **reservoirs** are needed to hold the water used to produce the electricity. Huge areas of rain forest, especially in Brazil, have been flooded to make way for them.

RAIN FORESTS AND GLOBAL WARMING

Global warming is the slow rise in temperatures on Earth. It is caused by greenhouse gases. These are gases on Earth that trap energy from the sun and stop it from being reflected back into space. Carbon dioxide is a greenhouse gas. Burning rain forests, like the burning of **fossil fuels** such as coal and oil, produces large amounts of carbon dioxide. It is thought to be a cause of global warming. Global warming is leading to the melting of the polar ice caps, rising sea levels, floods, droughts, and wildfires.

SOME PEOPLE TAKE PART I DEMONSTRATIONS TO RAIS AWARENESS OF GLOBAL WARMIN

Many animals are losing habitats because of global warming, including polar bears that live on the Arctic sea ice.

26

Rain forests remove carbon dioxide from Earth's atmosphere, and caring for them is one of the best ways of tackling global warming. Rain forests are sometimes referred to as the "lungs of the planet." Rain forests also play an important part in maintaining Earth's supply of fresh water. Rain forest plants release **water vapor** from their leaves, which forms clouds and eventually falls as rain.

Fresh water is very important. It provides people with clean drinking water. Deforestation affects how much fresh water we have.

RAIN FOREST RECOVERY

We can all help the rain forests to recover. Make sure that any rain forest products your family buys, such as bananas, carry a Rainforest Alliance Certified sticker.

Rainforest Alliance stickers have a green frog on them. These products have been made or grown while looking after the rain forest.

Look at the ingredients list on products. Try to avoid buying items containing palm oil.

PALM OIL COMES FROM THE FLESH OF THE OIL PALM FRUIT AND FROM THE SEED INSIDE.

If your family buys anything made of wood, check to see if it is wood from a rain forest tree. If it is, you could suggest something made from a different type of wood.

ECOTOURISM

Ecotourism is a form of travel that supports natural environments, such as rain forests. Local people can earn money by guiding tourists and providing places to stay and eat, rather than by cutting down the rain forests for farming.

CHARITIES

Many charities are trying to protect rain forests and the threatened plant and animal species in them. They aim to stop deforestation and to plant as many new trees as possible. They also work with local people to find ways of farming that give farmers a fair wage and that look after natural resources.

Ecotourism brings money to local people and allows tourists to enjoy the rain forests without damaging them.

Planting trees helps repair the damage done by deforestation.

UR FAMILY COULD SUPPORT A CHARITY SUCH AS THE WWF (WORLD WILDLIFE ND). YOU CAN FIND OUT MORE ON THEIR WEBSITE: WWW.WORLDWILDLIFE.ORG

FASCINATING FACTS

Some of the longest rivers in the world flow through tropical rain forests. Besides the Amazon, they include the Congo (3,000 miles/5,000 kilometers), the Mekong (2,600 miles/4,200 kilometers), and the Orinoco (1,336 miles/2,150 kilometers).

ORINOCO RIVER

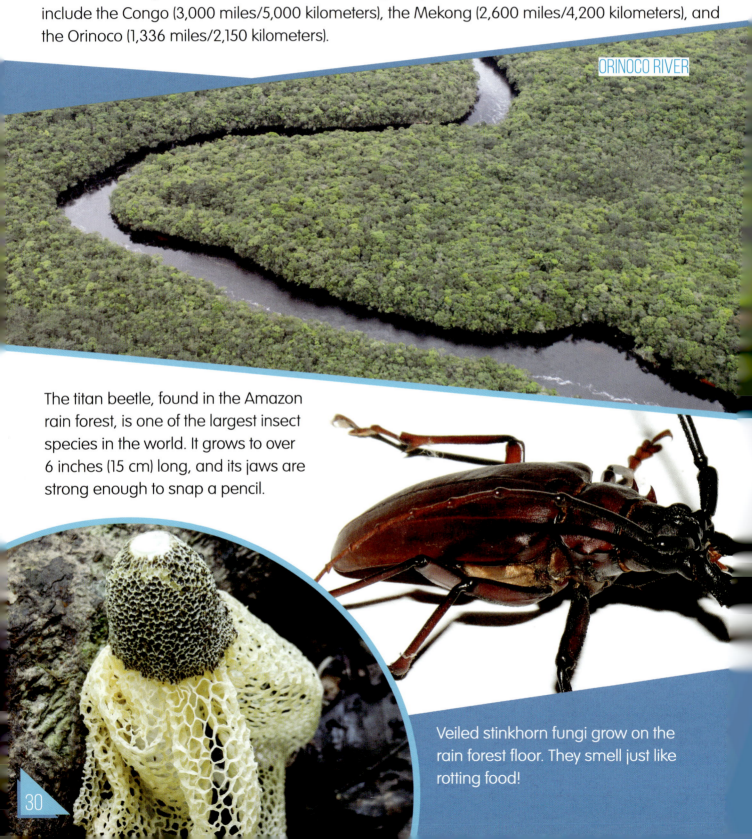

The titan beetle, found in the Amazon rain forest, is one of the largest insect species in the world. It grows to over 6 inches (15 cm) long, and its jaws are strong enough to snap a pencil.

Veiled stinkhorn fungi grow on the rain forest floor. They smell just like rotting food!

GLOSSARY

adapted	changed over time to suit the environment
algae	a plant or plantlike living thing that has no roots, stems, leaves, or flowers
camouflaged	using colors and patterns to blend in and hide in a habitat
carbon dioxide	a colorless gas found in the atmosphere and in the air that humans breathe out
cosmetics	treatments and medicines used to make someone look better
food chain	a series of living things that all rely on the next as a source of food
fossil fuels	sources of energy, such as coal, oil and gas, that formed millions of years ago from the remains of animals and plants
fungi	simple living organisms that are neither plants nor animals
habitats	the natural homes in which animals, plants, and other living things live
humid	air containing a high level of water; damp
mammals	animals that have warm blood, a backbone and produce milk for their young
microorganisms	tiny organisms, such as bacteria, that are too small to be seen with the naked eye
mosses	a type of plant that has no roots or flowers, and covers things like a carpet
nutrients	natural substances that plants and animals need in order to grow and stay healthy
predators	animals that hunt other animals for food
prey	animals that are hunted by other animals for food
reptiles	cold-blooded, scaly animals that have a backbone
reservoirs	huge lakes or ponds created by dams
species	a group of very similar animals or plants that can create young together
water vapor	water that is in the form of gas and below boiling temperature

INDEX

A
Amazon
- **basin** 25
- **rain forest** 5, 22–23, 30
- **river** 22–23, 30

B
birds 4, 7, 11, 16, 23

C
carbon dioxide 6, 26–27

D
deforestation 24, 27, 29

G
global warming 26–27
greenhouse gases 6, 26–27

H
habitats 5, 11, 14, 26

I
insects 4, 7, 10–12, 14, 17–18, 30

R
rain 5–6, 8, 14, 27
rain forests
- **temperate** 5
- **tropical** 4–5, 13, 22, 30
reptiles 4, 19, 23

S
sunlight 5–10, 12, 16, 18